Can YOU spot the rocket
hidden in the story?

For my dearly departed Dad,
who fuelled a young imagination
and let it fly.

Oisín McGann started writing and illustrating stories when he was about six years old. Most of those stories had to do with being out in space, or underwater, or ... well, anywhere but school, really. When nobody stopped him, he kept doing it and ten years later he ended up going to art college to learn how to get paid for doing it. Another ten years later, his friends and family started to realise that he was serious about this writing and drawing business and was never going get a proper job.

He is still at it ... and if *he* can do it, anyone can.

Oisín has written more stories about Lenny and his grandad – *Mad Grandad's Robot Garden, Mad Grandad and the Kleptoes* and *Mad Grandad and the Mutant River.*

Mad Grandad's FLYING SAUCER

Oisín McGann

THE O'BRIEN PRESS
DUBLIN

First published 2003 by The O'Brien Press Ltd,
20 Victoria Road, Dublin 6, Ireland.
Tel: +353 1 4923333; Fax: +353 1 4922777
E-mail: books@obrien.ie
Website: www.obrien.ie
Reprinted 2006.

ISBN: 0-86278-822-6

British Library Cataloguing-in-Publication Data
A catalogue record for this title is available from
the British Library.

2 3 4 5 6
06 07 08 09 10

The O'Brien Press receives
assistance from

Editing, typesetting, layout, design: The O'Brien Press Ltd
Illustrations: Oisín McGann
Printing: Bercker, Germany

CHAPTER 1

The Spaceship in the Paper

I was having tea and biscuits at Grandad's house when he saw the strange **advert** in the newspaper.

'Lenny, look at this!' he said.

There, in the paper, was a small ad. It read like this:

'Wow!' I said, imagining myself as an astronaut. 'Can we go and have a look at it, Grandad?'

'I don't see why not, lad,' he replied. 'I've always wanted my own **flying saucer**.'

Grandad wasn't like other grown-ups. Mum and Dad said he was a bit **mad**. He sometimes heard voices or saw things that weren't **really there**.

But he did stuff no other grown-up would do. Mum and Dad would *never* have taken me to look at a flying saucer.

We jumped on a bus and
went to the address in the advert.

CHAPTER 2

The Old Lady Alien

We walked up the path to the front door. There were **lights** all over the front of the house and the walls were painted **silver**.

Grandad rang the bell and the door opened. There, standing right in front of us, was an **alien**.

She was an **old** lady, but an alien all the same.

Normal old ladies don't have **blue** skin and **loads** of eyes that go all the way around their head.

'Ah, you'll be here about the spaceship,' she said. 'I'm Mrs Vamox. Would you like some tea?'

We went out into the back garden while she put on the kettle. And there it was, as real as you or me. A big, round, shiny **flying saucer**.

'I've decided to stay on this planet, because it's nice and quiet,' Mrs Vamox said when she brought out the tea. 'So I won't be needing my ship any more. What do you think of it?'

I couldn't speak, I was too **gobsmacked**.

Grandad gave me a look.

'We think it's great,' he said. 'How much do you want for it?'

And that was how we bought a spaceship.

Mrs Vamox showed us how to work the controls and then we climbed into the seats and the **glass dome** closed over our heads.

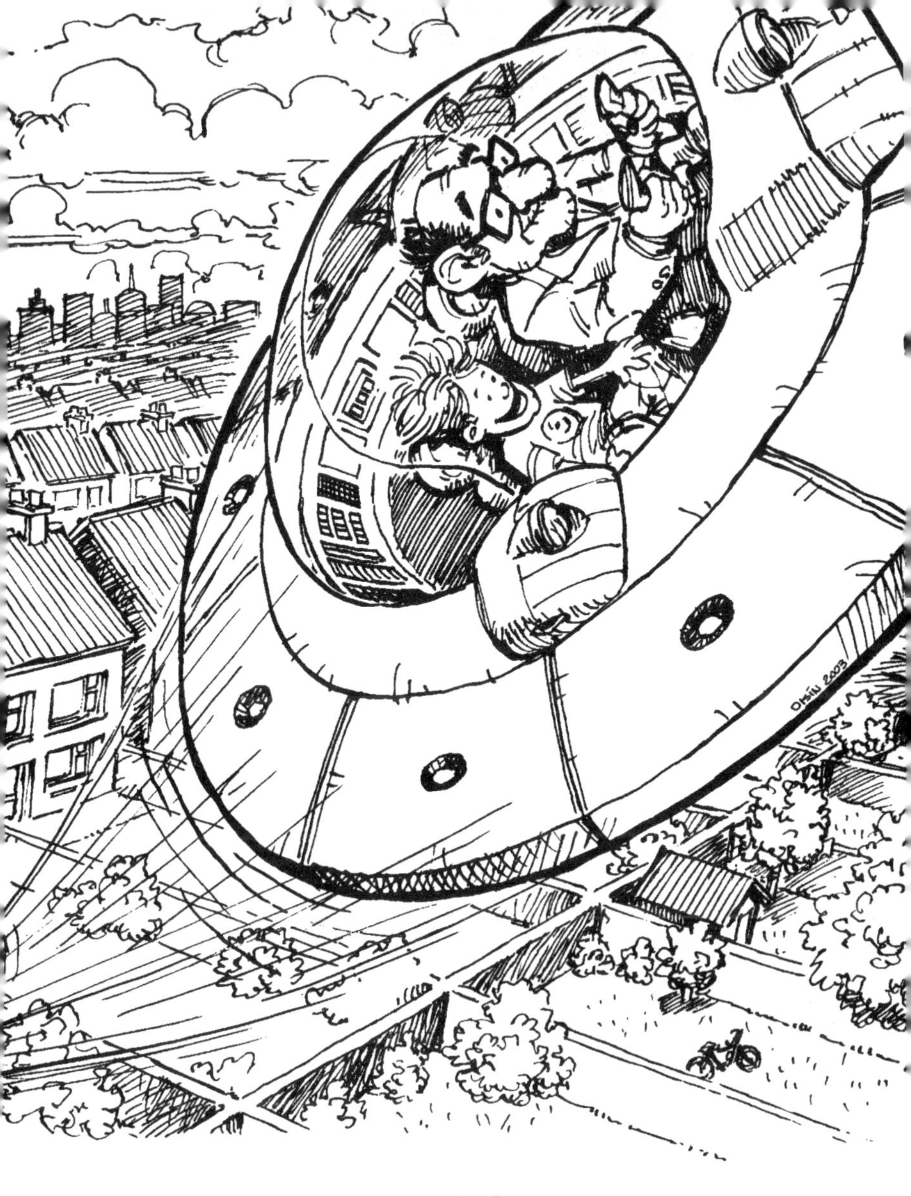

We took off and shot up into the **sky**.

CHAPTER 3

The Parking Guard

'Let's go into **space**,' said Grandad.

'Okay,' I said.

He pointed the spaceship straight up and kept going until all we could see were **stars**.

‘Wow!’ I gasped. ‘Look at all that!’

Grandad slowed down and stopped. We turned around and looked down at the **Earth**, a big blue ball below us. All sorts of weird **satellites** flew past us, spinning around the planet.

'I should have brought a **camera**,' I said.

'You can always bring it next time,' Grandad told me, 'but we need to go now. Your mother will think I've got lost in the city again. She'll be worried about you. We'll come again next weekend and have a **picnic** and everything.'

He was just starting the flying saucer up again, when a **big, mean-looking spaceship** flew down in front of us.

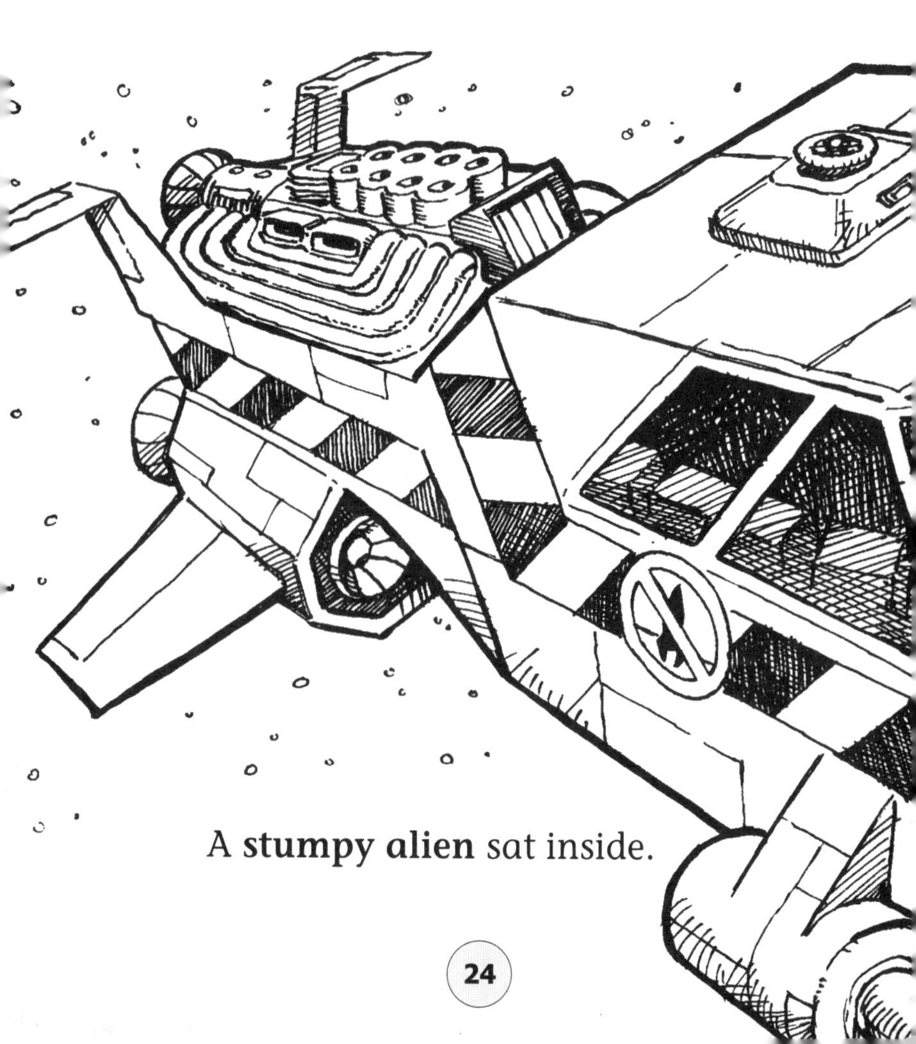

A **stumpy alien** sat inside.

He had **holes** all over his face and hands, and was dressed in a uniform that was much **too big** for him.

'You are not allowed park here,' he called out, 'not without **paying**.'

'Why should we pay to park here?' I shouted back. 'We're out in space.'

‘Oh, this isn’t just any old space,’ the alien shook his head. ‘This is **Parking Space** and I’m a **Parking Guard**. And you haven’t paid up. Do you know what happens to people who park without paying?’

‘No,’ I said, then wished I hadn’t.

‘They get **clamped**,’ the Parking Guard said, smiling.

He pushed a button on his control panel. Suddenly, a big, yellow, metal thing was fired from a hatch in his spaceship. It shot over to our flying saucer and stuck with a loud **CLANG**!

Grandad tried the controls.

The clamp was holding the spaceship in place.

'Lenny, we can't **move**!' he cried.

'Oh, you'll move all right,' the Parking Guard sneered. 'The **Collectors** are on their way. They'll take away that nice, shiny spaceship and you'll be walking home!'

'But how can we walk back to Earth?' I yelled. 'We'll fall and kill ourselves!'

'It's not my job to deal with complaints,' the Parking Guard said. 'Write to the **Complaints Officer**. I'm off, I don't like running into those Collectors. They're a nasty lot.'

He started his rockets and turned his ship around. In a flash, he was gone and we were left **alone**, stuck out in space.

CHAPTER 4

Splud Was Here!

'Grandad, what are we going to do?' I gasped. 'How are we going to get home?'

‘Now, don’t panic Lenny,’ he said, ‘we’ll think of something.’

I always get a bit worried when Grandad starts thinking too hard. You can see his face turn red and his **eyes** go in slightly different directions. I’m sure that’s not supposed to happen.

Just as I was about to start panicking, we saw a **satellite** coming towards us.

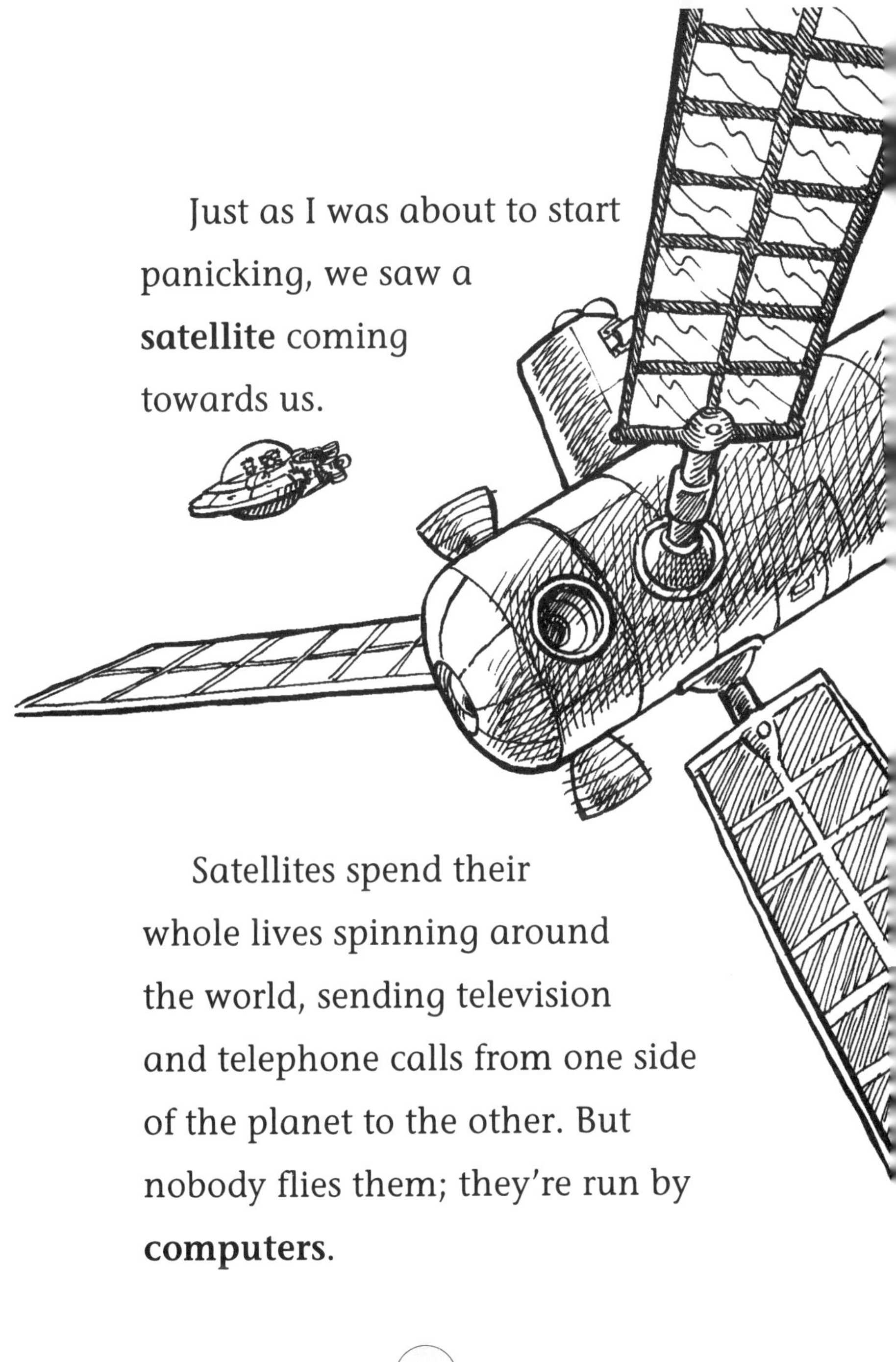

Satellites spend their whole lives spinning around the world, sending television and telephone calls from one side of the planet to the other. But nobody flies them; they're run by **computers**.

So when a **head** popped up from the other side of the satellite, I nearly jumped out of my skin.

It was a **thin, spindly alien** and he was crawling around on the satellite, holding a **spray-can**. He was writing with it. The writing said:

SPLUD WAS HERE!

'Oi! Splud!' Grandad shouted. 'Help us out here!'

The creature's eyes went so wide his **eyeballs** nearly fell out, and he ducked behind the satellite. Then he stuck his head out again to look at us.

'Who are you?' he called back. 'Are you the **Space Police**?'

'No,' Grandad said to him, 'we're humans, from Earth ... and we've been **clamped**.'

'That'll be the Parking Guards,' the graffiti artist replied. 'They'd clamp the moon if it stayed still long enough. I collect clamps myself. That's a nice one you've got there, that's a **Yellow Star-Crab Clamp**. I haven't got one of those yet.'

'It's yours if you can get it off our spaceship,' Grandad told him.

'It's a **deal**,' said Splud. 'I'll be there in a second.'

He let go of the satellite and **scrunched** up his face. Two jets of **green gas** shot from his feet and pushed him over to our spaceship.

He pulled out a strange **tool** and started fiddling with the clamp.

Just then, I looked behind us and saw a **huge, ugly spaceship** coming towards us.

‘Grandad, look!’ I said.

He turned and stared.

‘That must be the **Collectors**!’ he said. ‘Hurry, Splud!’

‘Right … right …,’ Splud muttered.

The huge ship sailed towards us. The front of it opened, showing us two jaws with rows of **giant teeth**.

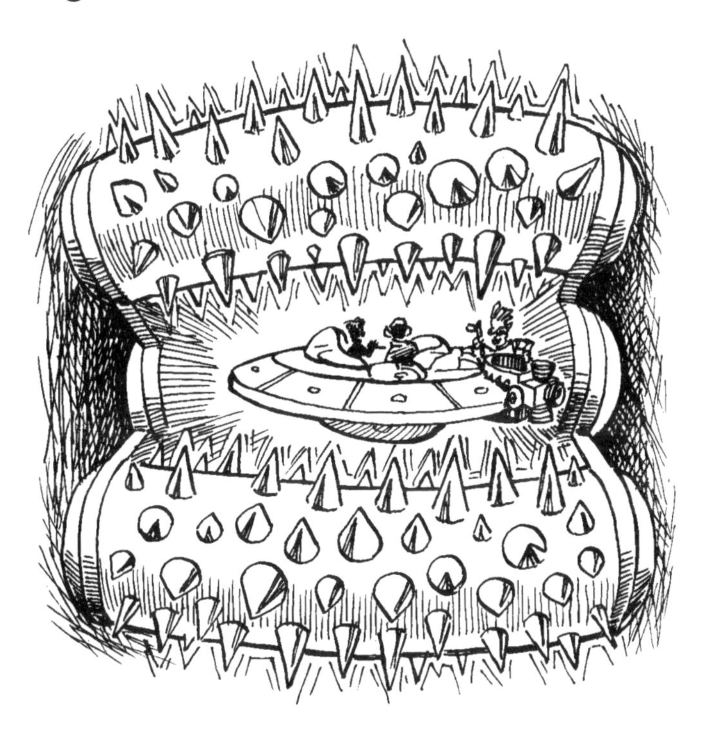

The Collectors didn't just collect – they **crunched**!

'Splud! Hurry up!' I yelled.

'I'm hurrying,' the alien replied, 'but it's tricky. Anybody got a **hammer**?'

I watched the Collectors' ship rush towards us. I could see the drivers smiling nastily.

'I'm getting out of here!' Splud yelled and **scrunched** up his face again, and the green gas started jetting from his feet.

The Collectors were almost on top of us.

'Grandad, come on!' I called and **grabbed** Splud's ankle as he took off.

'Hey!' Splud shouted. 'Let go!'

I caught Grandad's hand and we flew out away from the flying saucer.

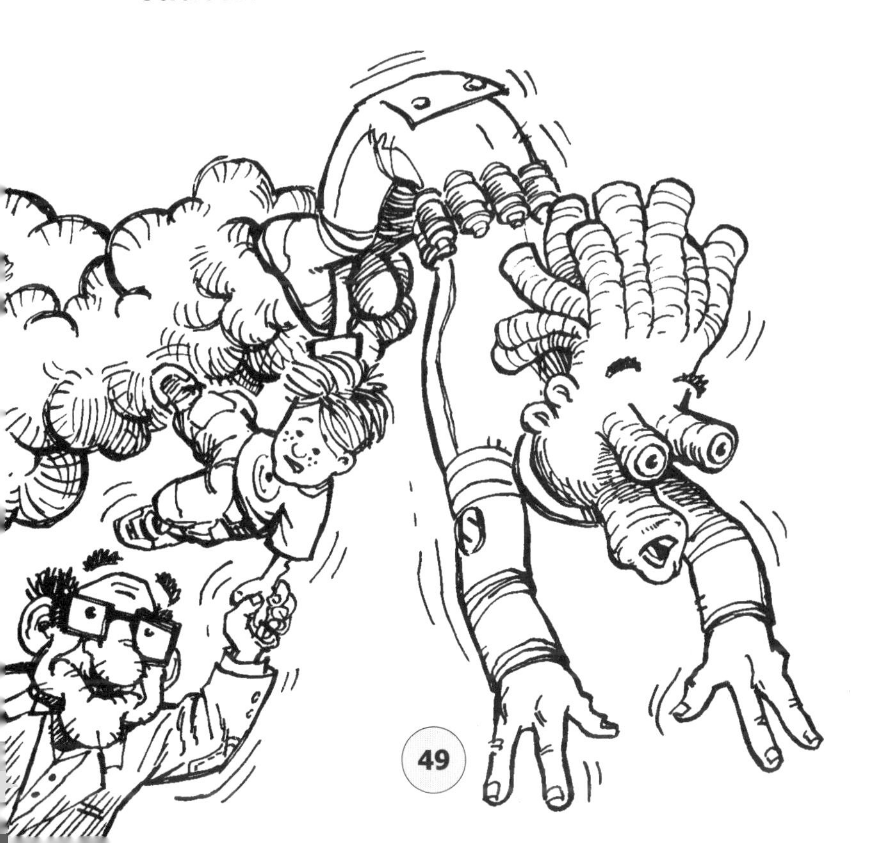

The Collectors' ship rushed in and bit into our flying saucer. It chewed and crunched it and swallowed up what was left.

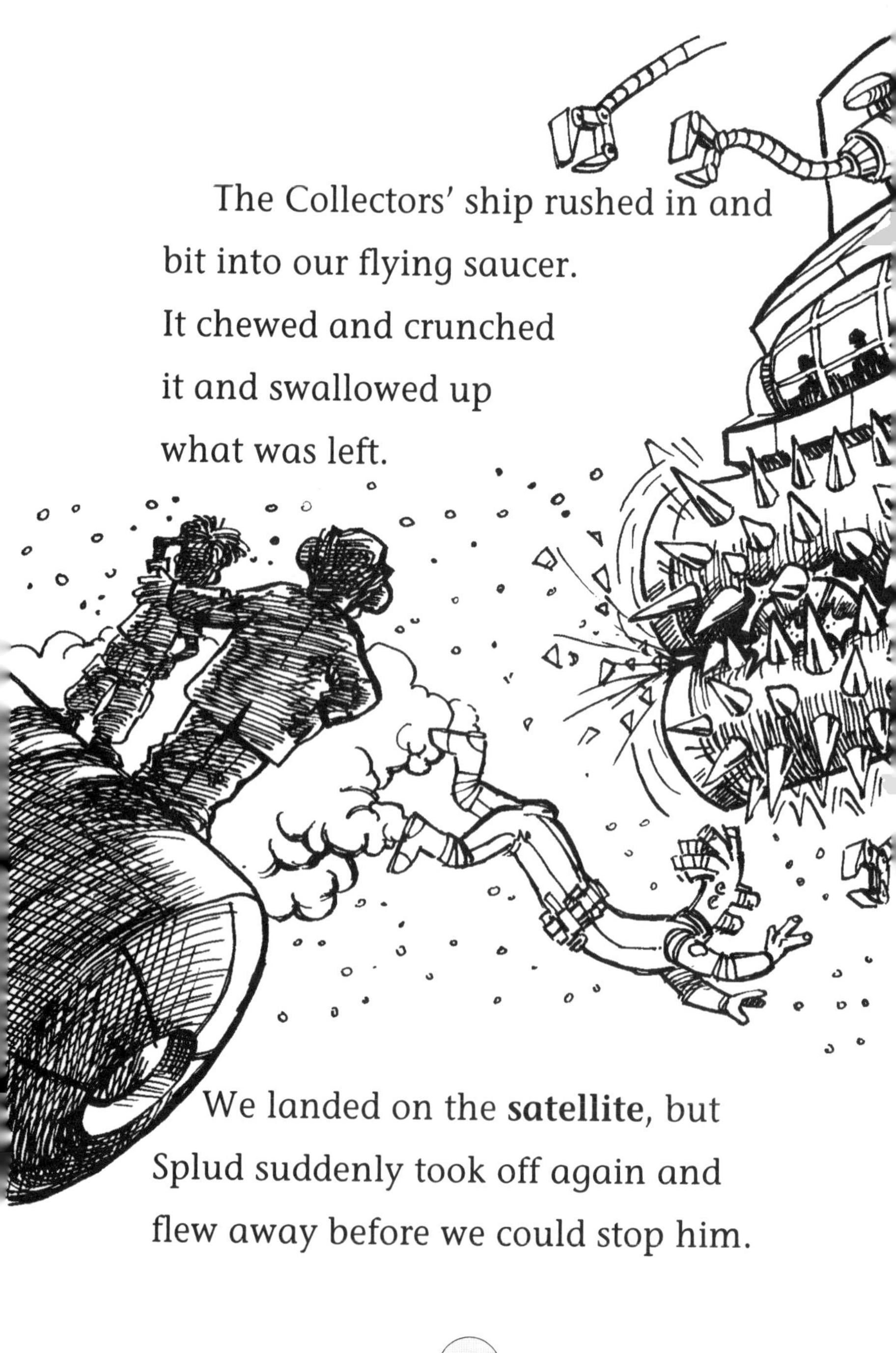

We landed on the **satellite**, but Splud suddenly took off again and flew away before we could stop him.

CHAPTER 5

Grandad and the Camera

'We're stuck again. What are we going to do now?' I said.

Grandad was looking at the satellite.

'I have an idea,' he said.

He started jumping up and down and waving. I thought he'd gone mad again. He jumps around like that when he's trying to change the TV channel with Dad's **mobile phone**. It can be a bit embarrassing sometimes.

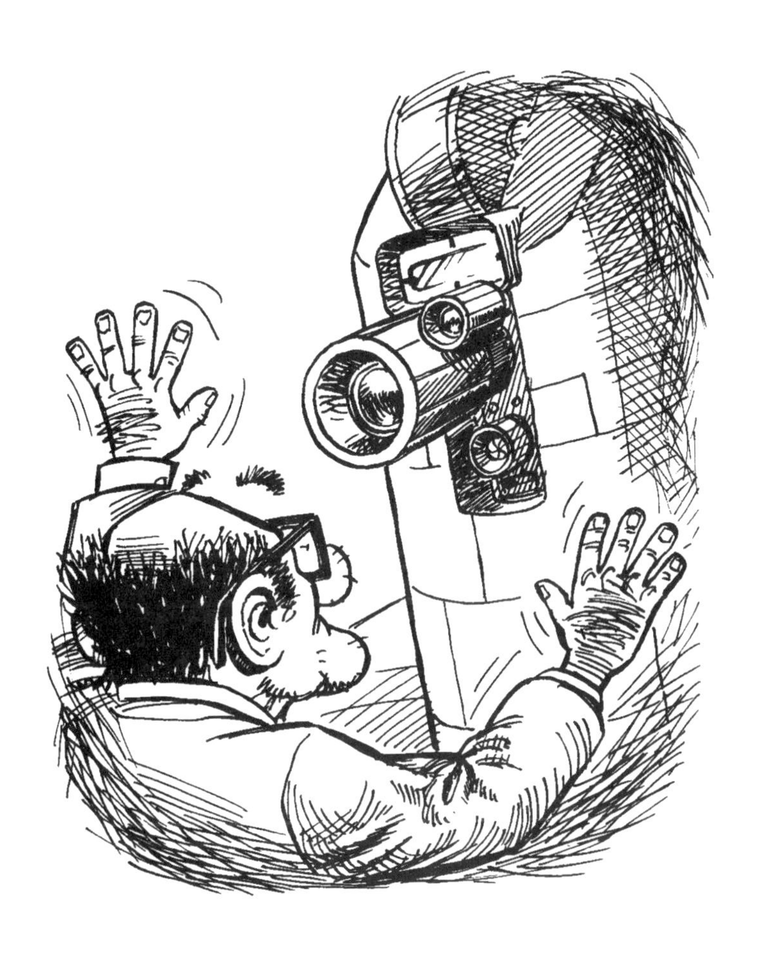

But then I saw what he was doing. It was a **spy satellite**, made for looking at people down on Earth.

We both stood in front of the camera and jumped up and down and waved.

At first, nothing happened, then there was a click ... and a buzz, and a hatch opened in the satellite.

A loudspeaker slid out. It crackled, and a voice said:

'Attention, Aliens! This is an Earth satellite! You have ten seconds to leave or we will shoot!

A laser gun popped up beside the camera.

CHAPTER 6

Glasses for a Laser Gun

'Ten, nine, eight …,' the loudspeaker was counting down.

'They're going to **shoot** us! Why do they think we're aliens?' I asked.

'Maybe the camera can only see things that are far away,' Grandad replied. 'So things that are up close are all **blurry**.'

'You mean like the way you see, Grandad?'

'Exactly, Lenny,' he said, tapping his **spectacles**.

'Three, two, one ...,' said the loudspeaker. Just in time I had an idea: 'Quick Grandad, give me your glasses!'

He handed me his spectacles and I held them up in front of the camera. It worked. Suddenly, the men down in Space Control on Earth could see us properly.

'Oh!' said the loudspeaker. 'You're **humans**! How did you get up there? Stay right where you are and we'll send up a **shuttle**.'

A few hours later, the shuttle arrived. The men looked disappointed that we weren't aliens, but they took us on board anyway.

The ride down was even better than the ride up had been, it was like a **roller coaster** with no slow bits.

Grandad nearly **swallowed** his false teeth.

So, in the end, we lost our flying saucer and never got to go into space again.

Nobody believed our story.

We could barely believe it ourselves. But then, whenever we thought it might all have been a dream, we looked at the back of Grandad's jacket and there, in **spray-paint**, were the words:

SPLUD WAS HERE!